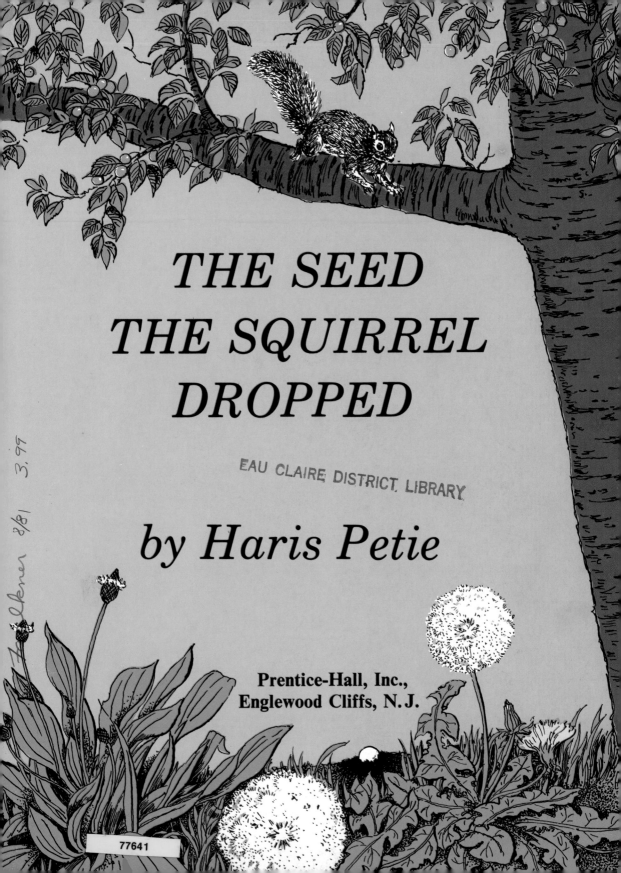

THE SEED
THE SQUIRREL
DROPPED

by Haris Petie

Prentice-Hall, Inc.,
Englewood Cliffs, N.J.

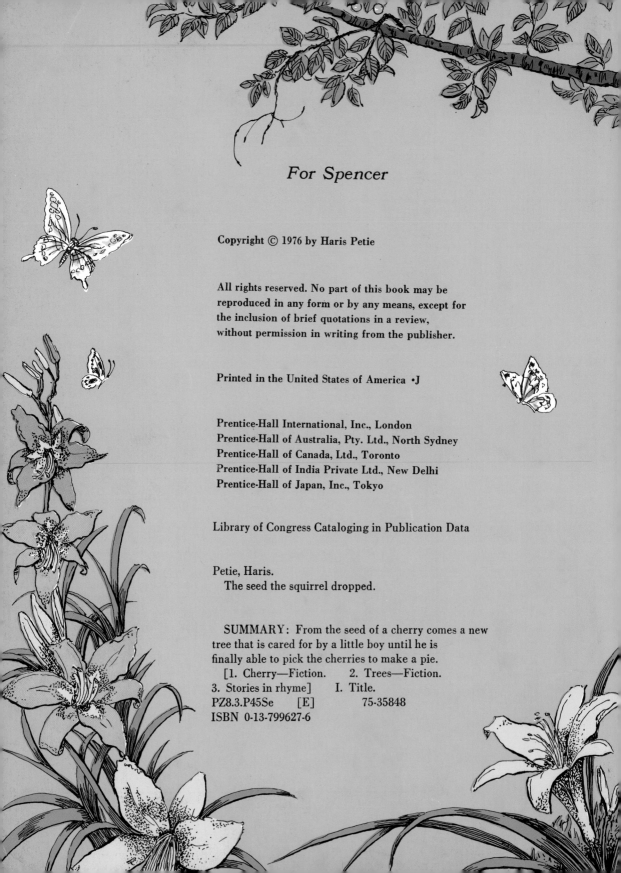

For Spencer

Printed in the United States of America •J

Prentice-Hall International, Inc., London
Prentice-Hall of Australia, Pty. Ltd., North Sydney
Prentice-Hall of Canada, Ltd., Toronto
Prentice-Hall of India Private Ltd., New Delhi
Prentice-Hall of Japan, Inc., Tokyo

Library of Congress Cataloging in Publication Data

Petie, Haris.
    The seed the squirrel dropped.

    SUMMARY: From the seed of a cherry comes a new
tree that is cared for by a little boy until he is
finally able to pick the cherries to make a pie.
    [1. Cherry—Fiction.   2. Trees—Fiction.
3. Stories in rhyme]   I. Title.
PZ8.3.P45Se   [E]   75-35848
ISBN 0-13-799627-6

This is the seed
The squirrel dropped.

This is the sprout
That grew from the seed the squirrel dropped.

This is the boy
Who found the sprout
That grew from the seed the squirrel dropped.

This is the spot
Where the boy set the sprout
That grew from the seed the squirrel dropped.

This is the rain
That fell on the spot
Where the boy set the sprout
That grew from the seed the squirrel dropped.

This is the sun
That beamed through the clouds
After the rain that fell on the spot,
Where the boy set the sprout
That grew from the seed the squirrel dropped.

This is the tree
That grew and grew,
In the sun and the rain
In the spot
Where the boy set the sprout
That grew from the seed the squirrel dropped.

These are the worms
That worked the earth
That fed the roots,
In the sun and the rain
In the spot
Where the boy set the sprout
That grew from the seed the squirrel dropped.

These are the flowers
That bloomed on the tree
With roots in the earth
That was worked by the worms,
In the sun and the rain
In the spot
Where the boy set the sprout
That grew from the seed the squirrel dropped.

These are the bees
All dusty with pollen
From the flowers that bloomed on the tree,
With roots in the earth
That was worked by the worms,
In the sun and the rain
In the spot
Where the boy set the sprout
That grew from the seed the squirrel dropped.

These are the cherries
All ripened and red
That grew when the bees
had dusted the flowers
That bloomed on the tree,
With roots in the earth
That was worked by the worms,
In the sun and the rain
In the spot
Where the boy set the sprout
That grew from the seed the squirrel dropped.

This is the pail
The boy filled
With cherries he picked
All ripened and red,
That grew when the bees
had dusted the flowers
That bloomed on the tree,
With roots in the earth
That was worked by the worms,
In the sun and the rain
In the spot
Where the boy set the sprout
That grew from the seed the squirrel dropped.

This is the tart
The boy baked
With the cherries he picked,
All ripened and red,
That grew when the bees
had dusted the flowers
That bloomed on the tree,
With roots in the earth
That was worked by the worms,
In the sun and the rain,
In the spot
Where the boy set the sprout
That grew from the seed the squirrel dropped.

Here is the boy
Eating the tart
He baked with the cherries
All ripened and red,
That grew when the bees
had dusted the flowers
That bloomed on the tree,
With roots in the earth
That was worked by the worms,
In the sun and the rain
In the spot
Where the boy set the sprout
That grew from the seed the squirrel dropped.

SPENCER'S CHERRY TART

CRUST

⅓ cup margarine or butter
⅓ cup honey
¾ cup shredded wheat
¾ cup wheat germ

Heat oven to 350° degrees.

Melt margarine in saucepan over low heat, strirring constantly. When it is melted, add honey slowly. Remove pan from heat. Stir in the wheat germ and then stir in the shredded wheat. Bake 15 minutes, Allow to cool while you prepare filling.

FILLING

2 cups pitted cherries
2 tablespoons cornstarch
⅓ cup honey

Put the pitted cherries in a sauce pan. Add the cornstarch and honey. Cook on low flame, and stir constantly, until mixture thickens.

Let the mixture stand for 20 minutes. When it has cooled, pour in pie crust.